ETERNITY RELATION

AWAITING HARVEST

SUMEET KUMAR

Made with ♥ on the Notion Press Platform
www.notionpress.com

Sumeet Kumar

Sumeet Kumar , A adult who experiences many phases of life , a well known writer and a writer of new era. In reality he is a writter as well as singer (as a hobby) and a standup comedian . Very exciting and interesting fact about him is that he is author of New era i.e. he starts his journey of writing at the age when he was going to schools to get the study . His streak of 100 books will be the great achievement for him in future. His some famous works i.e. Maturity Of Love (Genre - Love),Privacy For Dream (Genre - Middle Class), Army Squad ofLove (Genre- The Seperation of Army Love), 5 Days of

Love(Genre- Temporarily Love), Th e Endearment Of Love(Genre - Historical Era Of Love), Social Destruction Indo-Pak (Genre - The Story of The Love At The Time Of Division Of India And Pakistan), Middle Class Soul (Genre - The Dreams of Middle Class), The Accursed Kanatpur (Genre -The Horrific Story Of A Village), Wrong Number (Genre -The Suspenseful Physco Killer Story), The Secrecy OfDeadly Midnight (Genre - The Suspense About a Crime),Fragile Religious Of Death (Genre- The Death Of A TrustfulPerson), Nature Vs Science (Genre - The Future Battle Between Nature And Science In A Horrific Way), Generic Man (Genre - The Dream of I.I.T), The Unconsious 12 Hours(Genre - The Illusion At Stage Of Comma), The StrangeBurden (Genre - The Burden Of Love) , Her Existence (Genre- The Female Pain In The Society) , Jockstrap Prize (Genre -The True Story Of A National Athlete) , H Man [Hindi] (Genre - Superhero Tragic Story), H Man [English] (Genre - Superhero Tragic Story) , Maturity Of Love [Englsih] (Genre - Love) and many more are available on various geners on the offcial platform of Amazon, Flipkart and Notionpress. You can buy them from there.

Contents

Preface

It is the place where Lord Krishna was born and spent his early days. A famous centre of Buddhism in ancient India, the place was known for a great school of sculpture known as Mathura School of Art which flourished under the Kushana dynasty in the 1st century AD.

Vrindavan is the twin city of Mathura. It is one of the main locations in Braj Bhoomi region. It is believed that this is the place where Lord Krishna spent his childhood.

Many believe that He is. Legend has it that Krishna visits Nidhivan every night to meet Radha and other gopis. This is the place that witnesses the divine expression of love even today. At the center of Nidhivan stands a Radha-Krishna temple.

Inside Nidhivan, there is a little temple called Rang Mahal or s hringar-ghar of Radha Rani. According to folklore, Krishna visits here every night and adorn Radha with his own hands,It's not just a story it's a mystery..

Acknowledgements

Sumeet Kumar

Sumeet Kumar , A adult who experiences many phases of life , a well known writer and a writer of new era. In reality he is a writter as well as singer (as a hobby) and a standup comedian . Very exciting and interesting fact about him is that he is author of New era i.e. he starts his journey of writing at the age when he was going to schools to get the study . His streak of 100 books will be the great achievement for him in future. His some famous works i.e. Maturity Of Love (Genre - Love),Privacy For Dream (Genre - Middle Class), Army Squad ofLove (Genre-

ACKNOWLEDGEMENTS

The Seperation of Army Love), 5 Days of Love(Genre-Temporarily Love), Th e Endearment Of Love(Genre - Historical Era Of Love), Social Destruction Indo-Pak (Genre - The Story of The Love At The Time Of Division Of India And Pakistan), Middle Class Soul (Genre - The Dreams of Middle Class), The Accursed Kanatpur (Genre -The Horrific Story Of A Village), Wrong Number (Genre -The Suspenseful Physco Killer Story), The Secrecy OfDeadly Midnight (Genre - The Suspense About a Crime),Fragile Religious Of Death (Genre- The Death Of A TrustfulPerson), Nature Vs Science (Genre - The Future Battle Between Nature And Science In A Horrific Way), Generic Man (Genre - The Dream of I.I.T), The Unconsious 12 Hours(Genre - The Illusion At Stage Of Comma), The StrangeBurden (Genre - The Burden Of Love) , Her Existence (Genre- The Female Pain In The Society) , Jockstrap Prize (Genre -The True Story Of A National Athlete) , H Man [Hindi] (Genre - Superhero Tragic Story), H Man [English] (Genre - Superhero Tragic Story) , Maturity Of Love [Englsih] (Genre - Love) and many more are available on various geners on the offcial platform of Amazon, Flipkart and Notionpress. You can buy them from there.

CHAPTER ONE

MOMENTS OF LIFE

Moments are not so bad but some evidences related to them are very bad, when we are connected with their memories, then we leave ourselves bereft, every time I don a new face thinking that today's party is a glimpse of this morning ,Show some more new enthusiasm, but nowadays my character is also passing on the same path, where every habit of it is useless in someone's desire, I have not seen God's life very closely, but I definitely know that every blessing that I say is mine.

From the locality to my streets, there is Tehr caste. I had not thought that when God is the support of Mamt in the world, then something special will become special in my memories in that pride that I want to be associated with that pride, but we are short lived. Neither can I make my habit by returning the things of my past from a gathering, nor can I bring them to that gathering, my friends say that why my every car gets stuck on love,

And I bereft myself every time I hear this question, because my nature is not very strong that I can express it to them, why is every one of my writings remembered by them in Gujarati? Lord Vishnu had taken two incarnations. We all know one of them Shri Ram, and I can neither say nor do I have the character to say about him because he is the follower of the world, Hari Shri Krishna.

God is unique, every story is true, but it is heavier than life, I never thought that I am also a part of God's life, except my thinking Like steps which stays together for two moments and wraps after some time, that too in such a world, in the kind of locks I do everyday, but does not even want to give me its slip now,

I have never waved my hand in front of anyone, nor asked for water, but I go to the court every day, Sayad needs the party, if that person is mine, he is mine, then I do not need to go to his part and ask him. Ki Khairat Mangu, because every single story is related to him, he follows me, is karma, every tradition of God's world is Gujarati through him, he is Ram, he is Shyam, he is Mahadev, he is Hanuman.

I never consider him as a rahesya because every one of his knowledge is neither my power to go away from him nor his training can make me present with him, because I know that I belong to him, he is my Lord, faith is right against superstition. It is wrong, in this world such a habit of human race which never goes beyond humanity and humanity, these people are very bad in this world, they are very good, but we

We never talk, which is included in the gathering of these two, this Syed is present, when we go to Darga, we bow down, when we go to temple, we bow down, even when we go to Gurdwara, we bow down are so

Then when every impression of the blood of mankind shows a shadow of red colour, then why do people these days say that our religions are different, we are a different God, our faith is different, neither have we found such a thought nor do we have Neither religion nor faith, so who has done this?

CHAPTER TWO

LOST IN PEACE

It is not necessary for mankind to pass through the sacred thread of each and every religion, we have never been destroyed by that God who has never separated us from our own, neither from them nor from our own. Because in God's world, no parent can think bad about their children, nor can they give them the freedom of the grave, when a human turns to his mother's love, then no matter how many farukhs in front of him, why should he never Will not adopt because the religion that I talk about, and the humanity that I get at that time, no one else can give, even I do not know why in these things, because this is not a light to my religion, nor to my caste, then I Why am I telling about this? what people nowadays call Sanatana Dharma ,

There is no training of faith, it is continuous in its nature, its limits have not been fixed by anyone, nor can its limits be fixed, as much as I have heard about Ramayana and Mahabharata, both of them have training. This teaches us that if we leave our religion, go towards the evil, they make it a part of their life, they go ahead and consider it a part of their life, then it becomes a messenger of our death over time,come to the fore In Ramayana, neither Ravana's city was safe nor the sign of Kauravas, both of them fell in love because they had sacrificed their religion, this gives another lesson that if we sacrifice our humanity if so maybe the line of our life also says the same caste, it is not such a thing that our God is not alive in Ish Yoga, because if such a thing was there, then even this world would have remained the same without him, he existed then his every faith of mankind. I am not even saying that he has given us this life, but we cannot say that this life has not been given to us by the Unholy.

I am that child who can neither write each and every part of his knowledge with my own hands nor have I acquired so much training, with the passage of time I have also accepted that there is one copy of him everywhere no matter how many there may be but his Every illusion of the face gives me a new nature to live even today, this journey is not new for me, neither is the man who is a traveler whose desire has ended,

She is trying to distance me from herself, and I am not able to stop her even after doing six things, I know that she can destroy me a lot, but what should I do, I can't see any other reason to live, because I don't want her. I have also accepted that wealth of his. I am the public but the matter of my condo is telling me that if I get the insult of defeat, then say that Tabusam will never return, which once in my part is far away from me.

Has gone, if his charity and his love come again in my part, then I will get lost again in Syed, which I never started. The question is somewhere that where is he God? Where is this our God? But has anyone ever asked the question why we are looking for them, what is this curiosity that compels us every time we think about them, because if we had faith, we would have found them long ago. would have been

But this faith is questionable, and scientists have never tried to know it, because it is such a doctrine that neither science nor any other passion in the world can prove wrong, where there is faith, it is never a matter of iniquity. Where there is power and there is curiosity, the face of iniquity is vanishing everyday in its glory with a new life, have we ever asked ourselves why we have got this life?

If our God does not question us then we also have no right to ask him whether we are in this world or not. Dharma never gives us any knowledge nor does it teach us how to live because almost 200,000 years ago

When Agni was born to increase the life of man, then at that time neither the knowledge of Dharma was with us nor anyone had acquired its training, but at that time our God was definitely there, we had never worshiped Agni before that. It was seen that when the God of mankind was born on earth, then their faith came, then their religion and who was the creator of all these, our Lord, our God, whom we ourselves call Jesus.

Yes, Guru Nanak says, religions have imposed a curse on us, neither our God nor we ever belong to the caste of Sikhs, you separate from this religion and worship us.

CHAPTER THREE

RAM ALWAYS STAY IN HEART

*" RAM RESIDES
IN MY MIND
AS WELL AS
SHYAM RESIDES IN MY
BODY AND I
AM THAT CHILD
OF THIS WORLD
WHO HAS VISHNU
STAY IN HIS
EDUCATION ..."*

ADORE OF MA GANGA

Mother Ganga also exists here, Yamuna's dharam is also this council, so why not believe in that dharam, why not believe in its glory, the fire in which people catch their food for kud, that fire is also in the house of a Muslim. It is also present in the house of a Sikh and our Dharam whom we worship, it is present in my every ear, in my every body, the reason for my family is my hope to live,

The glory of which I am the only soul, I follow the world, without him neither the glory of any one can ever move forward, nor can a new story of Kishi Dharma be born.

If there is destruction somewhere in the journey, then try to move forward yourself, our Lord is with us all the time, hold on to your glory, your knowledge will remain with you if you walk with faith, neither in the age of God, nor in the age of God. To whom we believe, our Lord is present in every body of the one on whom we trust,

Our Lord is Brijman in every body of him, I believe that I will leave the journey but will come again in the next morning, my luck may not be with me but my hard work will always be with me, that too till the end of Jayshe's my

God Every body is together, in every faith and in every religion too...

This story is neither against time of dharam nor does it mislead anyone, it is just a beginning of that path which will promote the thinking of mankind, that too not towards faith, nor towards Muslim. Yes, I belong to Sikh, I belong to Kishi and Dharam, because, if you believe me, I am one for all and if you don't believe me, consider me as a child of my Lord Vishnu, who is lost in his glory and who Not religion, people believe in their faith and they also worship them.

CHAPTER FIVE

RADIANCE

"

ONE IN
LIFE
YOU AND
ME NEVER
REMIND ABOU IMMORTAL
MEMORIES
NOR EVEN
MIND ONCE TIME
NOR
AS IF
I ONLY HAVE
THAT RELIGION
WHOSE CLOUDS
ARE DARK
AGAINST YOU .."

CRIME BEHIND MATHURA

Some people live in such a way that it is okay if they are not hated, in the same way there are some stories whose fate we cannot decide, no matter what nature says, its fate never changes. When a writer expresses his feelings, that too by writing such a vast story, which has no limit, then his thinking stops there, but if his intellect is sharper than that. so it will never stop And if he is not there, then it is possible that his only safari should also be written on the same pages where his safari is done only by the dead and not by any common man. We never meet any witness in real, it is the illusion of God's world which connects us with each other, neither the limit of our love decides the relationship nor our relationship with anyone. We weaken to be with,Those are some compulsions that change the situation and take us on such a path in which some people say no to anyone and that the unconscious is aware. Let's do Safari, when you trouble a teacher, it is also necessary to stop him because with time his desire becomes more famous for someone else and if on time we If his alms is not returned, it is likely that he will throw himself into someone else's arms.

Well some things never have limits and nothing will. That lovers, we should neither try to join his journey nor request him to go to his party, because if we tell him our wish, then whatever happiness we have in the big party will be saved. Change will not take time.

Mathura Vrindavan

Banke Bihari 281121

(Uttar Pradesh)

What to say about Mathura, whose body is Sri Krishna Brijman, whose illusion is also an identity of glory. Love binds Kadar in me that we will never be able to get rid of it even after saying that, you all have not even competed with us, so let's go first, let us become aware of ourselves, then our story If it does not move forward, then like our aunt, its beginning will also appear as a suspense all the time.

By the way, our name is identified as Nandkumar Yadav, and our brother-in-law who is a very good person by profession, but before that he is a confectioner, it is not that he is not educated, because he has become a confectioner, I mean to say that there are some people who try to share their status by looking ahead, Ishqiye we have already tried to clear some things, our Bauji has an incomplete story which started from bihar and finished shape in mathura i mean to say It is said that Bauji also had big dreams since childhood and his hopes too, Bauji used to tell him to join the army, but our grandfather told him not to Said that you are the last lamp of our house, how can we let you go to the army, you tell me, and all the rest of his uncles also told him that see the principle, if you want to do something Do it but don't let you do this because you are the only lamp in our house He said no to Ishqiye Bauji, but his dreams went away from him at that time because he There were only lamps,Bauji did not stop even at this, those people had decided from childhood that even if they leave my dreams with me, I will never leave them, nor that love one day they will be hidden from everyone's eyes. Those people even tried to run away, but digging their luck was nothing special in themselves, the day when they decided that they would run away and fulfill their dreams in some other city, on the same day such a Fanna came to our house that his only friend whom he loved very much,

His name was maybe Harish Chaturvedi, but Bauji used to call him Chatur, now we do not know what is behind this, but he Does anyone know about the day Fanna came into his life? Because he was never told nor about his friends, means as far as I have heard about Harish uncle, he Ish is not in the world but the reason for his death and leaving the dreams of Bauji ,It seems to us that the reason for this is almost the same, but no one knows why they said good-bye to their army dreams.

CHAPTER SEVEN

HOLD MY SUSPENSE

If there were no dreams, there would be no hope, no light, she is the only one who takes our feet towards freedom, sometimes in the locality, sometimes on the road, sometimes in the streets with bare feet, whatever Bauji did, he found it right. But if I am Hotka in their place, I never give up my dreams of getting Sayad, because I do not know the wave of pain that I get when they break up, and if I am lost, then my world will be looted, well, I am my mother about I want to say something which I have never told her, she is my whole world and her husband too, means our brother-in-law too, I love them both so much that I can never think of leaving them, the reason is like this, Because there is only one safe place in his God and his world, where I do not ask myself to be safe, but I am safe, by the way, my world's Kamala Yadav is the goddess, from whose food even the aunties next to her come to learn new stories from her everyday,Caste, what to do now, like my mother, no one cooks food in the whole of Mathura, since childhood, I have been in some kind of bad condition and have no problem, because after Bauji, we are the only lamp in that house. The house where Nandlala Bhawan is, and I am not Krishna, but don't know why people call me Krishna instead of Nandkumar.

Well these things have happened which will continue to happen, but before that complete your story which is passed through reality, I was the only lamp in that house who neither had any dreams nor worries about the future because holding my hand I had my aunts to raise me and my aunts from behind.

His father means my grandfather, it is said that in whose house a woman is born, she is the symbol of Maa Lakshmi, although this is true, but not only Maa Lakshmi but also Maa Durga was born in my house. Because till today whenever I have faced any problem, they have supported me every time, well what can I say about my mother and aunts?

I could never know the sad things when I was in the love of my mother, but today that is not the case because because of one wrong decision of mine, I lost that world and her love too, I never thought that the boy who was mine Running away from the future, every day he will talk about the future and think about it, this thing is a bit curvy but it is true that I have never eaten with my hands, because sometimes the bauji used to bloom, sometimes mother and then my aunts, they There was an Ayesha heaven that I achieved while I was alive But I had never thought that because of me every wall of that heaven would become an object of Kishi Narg, and its people would become its slaves. Well, everyone's life doesn't have a happy ending, everyone knows this and everyone must have seen it in movies too, but in my life it was a happy ending, but after I left?

PROTECTOR

"I AM THE
KEEPER OF RELIGION
I M NOT
WORRIED
ABOUT UNRIGHTEOUSNESS
I AM MADE
OF HUMANITY
I DO NOT
CARE ABOUT
BRUTALITY ....."

DREAMY INTENSITY

I used to not like to study like that earlier, that means Bauji never forced me that why don't you go to study, but whatever I used to study, I used to understand it immediately and I used to get very good marks, if I can guess, then I was in my childhood. I am a topper since then, yes it may sound curvy to hear this, but what is the truth, even though Bauji did not force me for anything, he always used to say that if my dreams were not fulfilled, would you

Having fulfilled my dreams, I found this thing a bit emotional, but I did not know that it would become a pressure in my future, when I turned 18, Bauji did not give me any gift on my birthday, instead he Dreams handed over to me do not make sense, I am not talking about the dreams of soldiers, I am talking about the dreams of confectioners, and the day they were handed over to me, I had accepted that my ,How is life going to be in the future? Why the confectioner? Behind this also he had a training which he wanted to teach me, I do not want to learn in power, but I want to. I just want to live my life like this, without any effort and work, because those where is lack of money but we had money and I never said these things to my brother-in-law that day in front of him, and the next morning he did not send me to the place where he had seen his dreams, that too in the army. , But my mother and aunts were unaware of this matter and my grandfather too, why did Bauji do Ayesha, for what reason did I never question him, that means this story is also running smoothly, neither any sorrow nor any happiness at all. Life is going on average.

BLESSING OF LORD

*"KEEP ME FREE
FROM
THE LOVE
OF THE WORLD
AND I CONSIDER
MYSELF IMMORTAL IN
EVERY
ACT OF MATHURA
BECAUSE IN MY
KNOWLEDGE
SHRI KRISHNA
IS KEPT ...."*

RELATED TO PAST

Even if some memories go away with time, but they never leave behind, that too for the oppression that they never had, a person is aware of his bad and good condition all the time. Also his request to get someone or someone, She is always ready at that time, even if she does not get destruction in her part, love, sacrifice, friendship, relationships, all these are precious gems in today's world. The one that everyone is looking for, but its limit which stops a little bit, it cuts off their power and relationships from their own, then there is only one reason for that and that is wealth, but in my story there is no such Even charity was not clearly visible, so I asked him this question, why only at the end?

From the time I left Mathura, that city had become completely new to me, and I was in my own neighborhood and For the streets, Ayesha had become a human being whose nature was that of a traveler and Sayyid was also a witness whose wealth was handed over to his father's four, I have been living your life since childhood. I am living in happiness, then this tension, I am not able to rash these days, and why did Bauji call me Bihar?

What did he want to say, who could not tell me in the last moment, who was already unknown to me How the border is in the mist, nowadays every impression of his tears in my every hand is troubling me, I know that I am his own, yet why can't he be mine. I had come but I didn't know what to do, in other words, should I improve my condition first? once upon a time gold pond Pretending that they had become the moon by lifting the veil from the mystery about which I didn't even know properly, and why did Bauji say that you should first go to Bihar to meet Anant Chacha, who is this and my old house, Ma had said that I grew up here, meaning The copy of my birth and every memory of it is related to Mathura, then why did Bauji tell me that you definitely belong to me but you do not have the right.

Well, as soon as I went to Bihar, all my happiness had turned into sorrow, because as soon as he left, I met such a witness whose brain battery was down since a long time, and probably he had forgotten to charge it, And I didn't even have that charger with me so that I could solve each and every knot of his question according to Ushi, leave it to all of you to suffer so much, I don't have rash otherwise who will listen to my story, I am The day I went to Bihar, that day I met everyone Earlier it happened with an unknown witness who was innocent of heart and pot of mind, I did not know him but he told me that I know you very well, first So I didn't believe him but when he took Bauji's name and talked to me about each and every member of my family, he told me about them, then I knew that he was really me. Why the public on the public and why has he come to do this?

First asked us many questions, then when he stopped, I asked him many questions, and my first question was who are you? what is your name At first he was a little nervous, then blushed, and then his eyes He blinked twice then told him his name that I am Kabir, Anant Chacha has sent me to bring you, although we both were of the same age, but he was calling me brother again and again, and I am God. had silenced because I was not used to this, that day I had already understood two things from his words, the first is that I cannot live like this for a long time, and the second is that Even if I touch it, I will not stop, because where are the localities of Mathura and its memories and where are the words of Bihar which seemed to me, one Mathura where the prince of palaces lived and the other Bihar where he lived. Was going to live as a prince.

CHAPTER TWELVE

THE LAST WAR OF ILLUSION ?

I knew these things that something is going to change but I didn't know that it was going to change so much and my life which was like heaven in Mathura will turn into hell in Bihar, but somewhere or other I was quite desperate because the reason for the puzzle was that each and every memory of Bauji's childhood was related to Bihar, and secondly, when he did not give up on his dreams at the behest of Grandfather, then after Harish's uncle left. What happened to Ayesha that she left even her dreams which were very important to her?

I never want to stop but I had got a reason to stop, that too in the form of Harish uncle, but Bauji had said that he has passed away, I mean as far as I have heard about him Everyone had told me that he had died, but did not tell the reason for his death, and everyone told me that only after he left, Bauji said goodbye to the dreams of the army, but what He is actually Harish uncle whom I saw there is another witness who has become the apple of my eye, but the thing to do in my hair is that when I asked Kabir, is he Harish uncle? because i have their I had seen this picture many times before and could never talk to me about this in my eyes, but is this true of my hair even then? Means if he is alive then my brother-in-law asked me Why was it said that he had died long ago?

There were so many questions in my mind that every one of my instincts was telling me at that time what to do now? The whole balance of the mind was also badly shaken at that time, meaning could not be understood. That after coming to Bihar I would have to face not one but all, and among them what was troubling me the most was why did Bauji lie to me? and told me Why were you forced to come from Mathura to Bihar Some questions, if they stay away from where, then their place seems like a life, but when those who come closer and closer to us, they become aware of us, then they become Sardar for us, and for me at that time they The questions were changing my mind in such a way that I was not able to think anything, that means I was already bereft, but at that time even when I got drunk, I was still in the shadow of sorrow, probably this happened to me for the first time in my life. The question was in front and behind it.

I had missed it because when I came to meet my uncle, my wedding procession had taken place in him, that too of sorrow, because in reality he was uncle Harish's own brother and he was also a twin...

It means that earlier less turning points in my life have come to knock even more, that too in the gathering of happiness? What is happening with me? I didn't think anything at that time and first called Bauji but he They were not picking up the call, at that time my life was affected from both the sides, I could not understand that I am cry or laugh?

Ebony Of Soulmates

"*MY SOUL*
TOO UPSET
IS
MY DESIRE
TOO
ASTONISHED
HAVING MORE
CONDITION IN
WHICH
HARVEST
TO IN
DETERMINATION
I
HAD BEEN
THAT,S IT
MY
SUFFERANCE
THAT,S THE
MOON."

Climax

But it is said that where there is a great city of sorrows, that night of peace also comes and at that time when I felt sore, every one of my problems went away from me for some time, because when When he hugged me, I had forgotten everything at that time, even the memories of Mathura had gone away from my place for some time, because his sisters were giving me their feelings, when I was talking to them. When he hugged me, I felt elated that I have known him for a long time. But this happiness also became happiness for me when I met Kiran Chaturvedi, who was Anant's uncle, I mean Harsh was Uncle's wife, at first her words seemed normal to me. But when the untoward incident asked me to return? Then I could not understand her words at that time that what she wanted to say to me?

Because Kabir had taken him and gone before asking him something, and Kabir also did not tell me about himself at that time that he is Harish uncle's son only.

After meeting Kiran Aunty, it was a different world for me after listening to her, Uncle revealed to me at that time that he was a little sick, so he told her such things, when I asked the question, what did she want to say?

There are many questions where the desire to fade away is troubling me even more, I want to go on that journey, but every step of my step is a hair today, let's accept that leaving this journey incomplete I am going but beyond that I am leaving the beginning in this gathering,

my dreams and the happines of Mathura was not passed to Bihar memories but now it is special for me ,I never want to go away because it is my And the questions of which my enemies have insulted me like a cuff, every memory of it is a crown of happiness for me.